Mr Buggane, Dear

GRIM TAILOR

To the Isle of Man, our beautiful home. The place that embraced us with its lovely people and enchanted us with its culture. Thanks for the never-ending inspiration.

Grim & Luna.

31 OCTOBER

Strong winds, it all begins with the arrival of strong winds. The frightened sheep flee in panic downhill, scattering the herd as if it were cotton balls propelled by the furious blizzard hitting the Snaefell mountain. Behind them, a mythical monster emerges, a hungry Buggane on the hunt, tracking his prey.

The journey is just beginning for the magical hunter, but today has already been a long and fulfilling day for Betty and Johnny. Their cafe is closing in 15 minutes, and by now, hundreds of customers have enjoyed the magical season's traditional chants on this mythical island and the special Hop-tu-Naa pie that Betty bakes each year.

Betty says goodbye to their last customers using the light of a dying sunset while Johnny focuses on calibrating the radiator in the lobby.

"Honey, how much time do you think you need?"

"I have so much to do that it might take me a couple of lifetimes to finish the shortlist," he says and smiles sweetly at his partner. "About 5 minutes. Why?"

"The constabulary called; they expect a full-blown storm, like with snow and everything, in the next few hours.

They're closing the mountain road and advise us to go down, so I'm gonna send the crew home. I can clean the kitchen while you finish."

"Snow in October? Are you serious? Weather is mental nowadays."

"I know, that's what they said. So you betta hurry, sailor!"

"Aye, aye, captain," Johnny growls with his best maritime bark, and she can't help but smile at the man's wisecrack.

It isn't long before the couple climbs aboard their vehicle in the parking lot of the old building sculpted on the hill, as the snow piles up.

"Ready?" asks Betty, taking off her gloves.

"Are you crazy, woman? Your fingers are gonna freeze and fall off in this cold." Johnny fastens his seat belt and, without thinking, uses the rear-view mirror to take one last look at his cafe.

"I know, but with this weather, I want to dig my nails into the steering wheel on the way down; the storm turned out to be more violent than I expected—"

"Wait!" Johnny interrupts her with a severe tone while keeping his gaze fixed on the mirror.

"What's the matter?"

"I think… no, it couldn't be… I thought I saw something in a window."

"What did you see?" Betty twists in her seat to look back, and a light inside the cafe turns on as she turns.

"It was something that looked like a small mask," answers Johnny, dead serious and with an exaggerated grimace of terror.

"Can you imagine?" she says as she tries not to laugh at Johnny's grimaces. "Some family gets home in Castletown and don't realise that they left one of their children in the cafe."

Now Johnny is the one struggling to maintain his terrifying grin amid his partner's good humour. "And meanwhile, the lad is hiding behind a sofa, and as soon as he stops hearing voices, he freaks out and starts running around flipping switches."

"If we don't handle this well, we'll be featured in tomorrow's newspaper."

"Does that mean we have to take this little kid to his house?"

"Of course! But we gotta find him first."

They unfasten their seat belts begrudgingly, and as the couple opens their vehicle's doors, the blizzard surprises them. It slaps the car with sudden intensity and mercilessly rips the doors from their hands and the vehicle's cabin, sending the pieces of metal flying a few meters down the hill.

"Something tells me we're not going down the mountain on this!" jokes Johnny, trying to raise his voice over the noisy storm spitting snow onto their faces.

Betty sighs and looks back at her husband through her foggy glasses with a tired and resigned expression. Within seconds, they open the cafe's doors, setting foot again in a place where they had just been, but that somehow feels completely different.

The gigantic restaurant filled with vintage bikes and puffy leather armchairs has a distinct and captivating personality in the dark. The only light on is in the lobby, shining on the golden inscriptions inked on the black walls, a microcosmos of scribbles illustrating the artistic effort of the local clientele.

"Why is the log burner open in the vestibule? I can see the embers inside; that's dangerous!" Johnny jumps into action, but before he can close the door, he finds three half-eaten pies waiting atop the stove. The place almost looks as if the cafe owners, fleeing the lousy weather, suddenly interrupted a private party.

"I cleaned this room before we left... Could it be thieves?"

"Nah, come on! What could someone want to steal from…" he trails off, shocked by a terrifying thought and takes off, running to the inside of the building, screaming, "MY BIKE!!!"

Before Betty realises she's alone, she hears a strange sound coming from the kitchen. With no escort, she investigates on her own, yawning quietly. She opens the door, shuffles her weary feet, and slaps the switch, turning on the kitchen light.

Johnny, for his part, bursts into the dark workshop, jumping like a daring ninja, ready to fight for his life and bike. Yet the only thing that takes his breath away is the sighting of his beautiful sidecar motorcycle, tempting him with promises of speed and freedom. As the man sighs deeply with relief, he hears a snoring noise coming from his toolbox inside the workshop.

"Oh no, please don't be a long tail, don't be a long tail," he mutters, convinced that he doesn't have the will to catch a rat right now, much less the heart to put it outside in this weather. Johnny takes a pair of glasses out of his pocket, hangs them over his nose, and bends down to look inside the open toolbox. What he finds inside doesn't make the slightest sense or isn't compatible with the laws of nature that this human knows.

In the kitchen, a harsh snore makes one of the pantry doors throb, and a thin cloud of flour comes out of the cabinet next to Betty. A chill goes down her spine as she grabs a rolling pin with one shaky hand and opens the dusty pantry with the other.

"Bets? You have to see this!" Johnny storms into the kitchen, carefully nesting something small in his hands, shaking with excitement.

"Let me guess…" Betty turns around to meet Johnny, and she's also carrying something impossible with her, biting her fingers affectionately. "What are they?"

"I'd say baby pigs, but when was the last time you saw pigs with wings?"

"Forget about their wings; what about their crowns?" says

Betty, referring to the small silver crown that floats magically over the head of each of the two little winged pigs playing with their fingers.

"Right?! Look at this." Johnny holds the beautiful creature with one hand while pinching the tiny crown with the other and lifting it slowly. The unknown force that keeps the floating crown connected to the little pig effortlessly lifts the creature that doesn't realise it, almost like a kitty when its mother carries it by grabbing its neck. "How's it possible that they don't weigh anything?"

"Leave the little ones alone!" Behind them, a raspy voice vibrates with an almost metallic resonance, barking orders into their ears from a work table.

Betty and Johnny shrink from the fright and twist to look at the table, trying to find the owner of the determined voice. But what they see is a roll of foil floating in the air, pointing one of its hollow ends directly at their ears.

Betty moves her face closer to the floating tube with uncertainty and then speaks into it, masking her voice with the same metallic resonance the phantasmagorical, demanding voice has.

"He—hello?"

"Pleasure to meet you. What are your pronouns?" Johnny is inspired by Betty's natural courage and asks something to the void, using this cardboard tube as a magical intercom.

"Me? Well… I'm the terrible Buggane, and those are my Fairy Pigs. So I order you to let them go at once!" The voice that responds using the foil tube as a megaphone sounds a little less sure of itself, almost like an innocent child improvising lies.

"Well, you have a healthy ego. I mean, who calls themself terrible?" Johnny uses humour to deal with the paranormal event, as the playful little pig escapes his grasp. It defies gravity, effortlessly walking on the human's arm and over his shoulder, then goes to nest on his jumper's hood.

The beautiful dusty Fairy Pig playing with Betty gives her an idea, and she turns to look at the open cabinet from which she rescued the little magical creature.

"Don't toy with my patience, mortal fool!!!" roars the invisible entity, making the foil wrapping the tube vibrate with intensity.

Despite the threat, Betty reaches out in a fluid movement, putting her hand in the cabinet and calmly digging up a fistful of flour. "The power of Christ compels you!" yells the woman as a shower of flour falls on the entity throwing a tantrum.

Suddenly, teeth and the open jaws of a creature making exaggerated faces become visible, and Betty and Johnny scream in horror. The beast roars then coughs flour, and with each involuntary spasm, the camouflage turns on and off, like a chameleon with paranormal hiccups radically changing colours in a snap.

"Aaaagghh, Twoaie, you blew it!" whispers somebody from above the fridge.

"I told you she was gonna lose her marbles, didn't I tell you?" says a third invisible entity, laughing behind the humans entrenched behind a baking tray.

"Girls! Stop taking the piss out of Twoaie; that's how we ended up in this trouble in the first place," scolds a fourth voice. "If The Howl realises the pigs are lost, ooooooooh, things are gonna get bad. I'm speaking of scorched ground, fire from heaven striking with lighting."

"Alright, alright…" says Twoaie, walking calmly on the kitchen counter towards Betty and Johnny as she wipes flour from her eyes. "Mortals! We're short on time, so I'm going to be blunt…" says the tiny brown sheep.

"Is that… a tiny Manx Loaghtan!?" mutters Betty, trying to understand what she sees.

"When was the last time you saw sheep walking upright on two legs, giving the time of day?"

"The same day we saw pigs with wings and crowns! If she's not a Loaghtan, what else, then?"

"I don't know, maybe it's an interdimensional creature, using a physical interface familiar to our brains? We might as well be talking with a steak and ale pie walking on two legs."

"Ok, no more Doctor Who for you for a while. Let's ask."

"Ok, but don't blame me if we end the night inside a flying saucer."

"Little one! Who are you, and what do you want?"

"The pigs! I thought that was clear by now; we need to find and collect all the pigs and fast!" screams another Loaghtan sheep, becoming visible as she throws a tantrum and stomps atop the refrigerator.

"Shiar, mate—cough, cough—calm down…" says Twoaie, coughing up the last bits of flour lodged in her throat.

"Oh great! There's two of them!" says Johnny, feeling surrounded.

"My name is Twoaie, and my sisters and I are looking for a litter of fairy pigs lost during the storm. Our job is to reunite the wee ones with their mother, and their track brought us here! The delicious aroma of your pies attracts the attention of mortals and divine alike."

"Lovely to meet you, Twoaie. My name is Betty," she says with cheeks reddened by the compliments, "and that's Johnny. How can we help you?"

"A pleasure! The grumpy one denting the fridge is Shiar; sorry about her."

"Nah, don't worry. No big deal, nothing that a good polish can't fix."

"Oh, so you think I'm denting the humans' toys?" Shiar sits on the refrigerator top and opens the door, letting them see the disaster area inside the refrigerated box. "Then let me introduce you to Heear."

The stubby little sheep covered in crumbs freezes in place inside the fridge. Yet, her jaws keep in perpetual motion as her hoof continues to carry baked beans into the food grinder that Mother Nature has installed under her nose.

"As you heard, the girl with the sweet tooth is Heear. If you are ever near her, don't stop blinking. She could mistake you for food and try to eat you," says Twoaie as Heear greets the humans with a mouth full of beans and an innocent gesture. "And finally, this is Jiass…" Twoaie points her hoof towards the kitchen sink, but it doesn't seem like there's anybody there. "C'mon, Jiass!"

"Nope!" mutters the fourth creature, refusing to remove her camouflage. "No thanks, I'm fine like this. I don't trust humans. I've heard the stories; they're meat-eaters!!"

"Oh, come on… don't judge. Everything's fine; you can let them see you. I'm sure these two humans aren't bad people, regardless of what they eat."

"Ok, ok… but if you try something, I'll ram your knee with my horns, humans!" The fourth Loaghtan sheep finally becomes visible, but Betty and Johnny can only see her eyes and horns peeking out shyly as Jiass insists on staying entrenched in the sink.

"Better than nothing, I guess! My friends and I have an extraordinary task, and we are in a predicament."

"Agh, enough with the big words and long stories," says Shiar as she jumps down from the refrigerator and lands in the kitchen next to Johnny. Then, she catches the man's cheeks between her hooves and confronts him up close. "We are the four cardinal points, the shepherds of this island, and we need those fairy pigs! Or else, The Howl will smell them, find us, and devour us all!"

"No, Shiar, no! Let go of the human's face!"

"What is The Howl? Maybe we can help or at least do something about it," says Betty, petting the pig purring above her head.

"No disrespect, but there's nothing a mortal can do to deal with it. The Howl is one of the many guardians." Shiar releases the man's cheeks and focuses his attention on Betty. "Like it or not, we're all connected."

"Guardians!?"

"Yes, guardians of the island's secret gate, the passageway between kingdoms," says Heear, leaving behind a trail of baked beans, mushy peas, mash and cake crumbs that she's attempting to carry out of the fridge.

"I'm not sure I follow… wait, I think I have something in the lost-and-found box that can help you… some kid left it here a couple of years ago; I don't think anybody needs it. You can have it so you can carry a little more with you."

Heear's eyes light up like stars as Betty helps her store food inside the colourful backpack that looks disproportionately big as it hangs on the little sheep's back.

"Loooooot!" Shiar's fury dissipates when she sees the lost and found box filled with potential treasures. Without thinking twice, she jumps inside it, rummaging through items forgotten by diners over the years.

"Girls…"

"I'm still not sure I understand what's going on here," says Johnny, fascinated with the antics of the four Fairy Sheep, "or understand who or what this 'Howl' is. Is it friend or foe?"

"The Howl is more like… hmm… like a magical custodial mechanism; it's no friend or foe. It's kind of cold, emotionless, regulatory and too powerful for my liking," says Twoaie, struggling to explain the concept.

"GIRLS!!!" Jiass leaves her trench, raising her voice with concern and finally making herself heard. "Girls, something's coming; I can feel it."

"It's true, you're right. I think I can hear it coming, too." Shiar emerges from the bottom of the lost-and-found box with her neck wrapped in a large TT scarf and a beanie on her head that's immediately stolen by Twoaie.

Slowly, everyone hears the grinding of sharp claws engraving cuts into the emergency door glass at the back of the cafe. The group inside the restaurant becomes speechless as they tiptoe out of the kitchen, trying to peek down the hallway that leads to the emergency door suffering a slow death from a thousand cuts.

Before the bulk of the group can get to the hallway, Heear is already there, leaning against the corner, glancing down the hall and at the emergency door. "Oh, good news," she says, turning around calmly while stuffing her mouth with chips. "It's not the Howl." She then sticks her arm inside the backpack, looking for something sweet, but what she rescues from the bottom of the bag are an old music player and its headphones.

Twoaie catches up with Heear and finds her biting the music player. She pushes her out of the way and discreetly peeks into the corridor. "Hmmm... this isn't exactly better, girl. It's just... different." Within seconds, everybody is peeking out, discovering the bad news on their own. "I think it's a Buggane."

"Dear, please remind me to repair the external lock on that door," jokes Johnny, who cracks a joke despite the terror freezing his body.

"Yeah, sure, I'll remind you. I guess it's nothing that a good polish can't fix," she says, smiling with a nervous gesture, continuing the joke that started in the kitchen.

The Buggane bursts through the emergency door as if it wasn't there, demolishing the door's metal frame and making glass fly into the corridor. He growls as he walks into the cafe, irritated by the cold and the storm.

"What a beautiful day; finally, Hop-tu-Naa is here,
Bringing the kingdoms closer with cheer and a little fear.
But something else has crossed the magic path; I can smell it in the air,
It smells like little fairy pigs, like a fab tea time, I swear!"

The Buggane bursts into the restaurant area with his nose held high, sniffing the snacks hidden in this place's nooks and crannies. Sheep, pigs, and humans hide under the counter as they hear the predator moving chairs and tables, and for a second, everyone holds their breath, feeling him approaching. They can hear the Buggane's hungry gut grumbling against their backs on the other side of the counter as his saliva drips into the cash register above their heads.

The escapists use all their concentration and physical energy to not produce any sound while breathing as quietly as possible. They wish their hearts would stop beating for an instant so they could go unnoticed by the mythical creature's jaws.

In that agonising moment, stabbing them with anxiety, Johnny looks at his feet, distracted by the sensation of something pulling on his shoelaces. The playful sound between Johnny's feet becomes increasingly louder until everybody's eyes move to the floor to find a new fairy pig playing with the shoelaces, almost like a kitty entertained with the shoestrings.

Johnny nods at Twoaie, suggesting that she catch the little pig. But the scared sheep refuses to move and touches Shiar's shoulder, inheriting the rescue task with a silent grin. Shiar raises her hand and turns, looking to transfer the job to her closest sister, but Jiass is already making aggressive gestures pointing towards her horns while articulating words with her lips without producing a sound. "Don't even; I will ram you!"

This is how the clueless Heear, playing with the music player, receives an elbow to the side and, without thinking twice, she springs into action. Dragging the bundle filled with edible goods, she approaches the little fairy pig. But, instead of catching him, she sits next to him and calmly munches on the laces on Johnny's shoes, as if the human had cordially invited her to savour the taste of his boots. Ironically, the little pig gets bored when Heear swallows the shoelaces. With no intervention, he climbs inside Heear's backpack, nesting inside it, using a pulled pork pie as a pillow.

Suddenly, Heear lets out an inter-dimensionally offensive

reverberating burp that rattles the glassware surrounding them, culminating in aglets shooting out of her throat and bouncing off the wall. The hunter, alerted by the commotion, darts toward the counter, his sharp claws raised high, ready to maul whoever is there with his talons.

Just before he reaches his victims, he feels a shooting pain in his wide-open eyes caused by the belched aglets that have bounced off the wall and have gone right into his eyes, making him lose focus for a few seconds. This distraction is enough for the group to restart their engines, sneak out of the kitchen and jump into the movie theatre inside the cafe. The enraged Buggane leaps behind the counter, bursting into the employee area.

"Is there someone else here? I can feel it in my bones...
Are you making a fool of me? I'll make you eat stones."

The group of escapists desperately crawl between the cinema seats to run away from the Buggane. As Jiass crawls for her life, she finds another fairy pig sleeping under one of the theatre's airline seats and scoops it up like a baby.

"Heear, let me put this little guy inside your new backpack. Heear...? Oh no, girls, I can't find Heear! I think we lost her!"

Utterly oblivious to the situation, Heear is on her way to the bathroom, putting on a show. The little fairy sheep finally understood how the music player works and turned the hallway to the bathroom into her catwalk, dancing uninhibitedly with a pig that accompanies her fluttering happily around her. Together they dance as if there were no tomorrow, leaving behind a trail of crumbs that doesn't go unnoticed by the Buggane, who follows the food and moves away from the terrified group, spying on him from behind the cinema door.

"Who is responsible for all this senseless waste?
Only humans can have this lack of good taste.
You don't understand my traditions for Hop-tu-Naa,

humans,

But this is important to us bugganes.

Once a year, magical creatures can wander into this kingdom,

That means that one night a year, we, the hunters, have a window."

The song blasting into Heear's ears through her headphones ends along with her impromptu dance as she and the pig reach the bathroom door. Right that second, the sheep notices the trail of food that she is leaving behind and the Buggane in the distance, sniffing, following the crumbs, his hungry stomach growling and echoing on the walls. Heear and the fairy pig realise the danger that has them trapped and, with no other choice, run into the bathroom before the Buggane can see them.

Inside the bathroom, Heear comes across the little boy forgotten by some tourist family, engrossed in making bubbles with the hand soap for a fluttering, flying pig to burst.

The Buggane picks up speed as he follows the trail to the bathroom at the end of the hall, and inside it, Heear doesn't mess around either. She grabs the magic pigs with one arm, the smiling boy with the other, and runs toward the door.

Suddenly, the Buggane kicks the bathroom door, tearing the metal sheet from its frame and turning it into a giant popcorn-like twisted heap that shoots against the back of the bathroom, demolishing the bubbling sink. Then, he bursts into the bathroom claws-first, carving the door frame with his talons, ready to fight with his food if necessary. Fortunately, in his impromptu attack, he doesn't realise that Heear is hanging from the wall like a spider, holding herself with all four hooves against the upper corner of the bathroom just over the door.

Heear bears responsibility for all the living and edible things inside this concrete crate and tries her best not to fall on the Buggane, but by the time he reaches the farthest wall in the bathroom, Heear can't hold on any longer. She feels as if the boy on her shoulders suddenly weighs a ton, and her little legs shake as she loses grip on the walls that make up the corner of the room. Inevitably, she slides down the walls and begins to fall behind the Buggane.

Right on cue, the two little fairy pigs catch Heear's front hooves and fly, turning a tumultuous fall into a clumsy but silent exodus. In an awkward act of escapism, the little pigs do their best to bear the weight of the sheep who saved the child from falling by catching him with her back legs. The boy experiences the luxury of flying while the sheep's legs support him comfortably around the waist, so he opens his arms and moves as if swimming in the air over the corridor covered in food crumbs.

The hungry Buggane continues rummaging in the bathroom, demolishing everything in his path, while the flying pigs escape. It's not long before they can no longer carry their heavy cargo and crash into the multiple sacks of fresh potatoes stacked near the lobby.

"Let's play a game of hide-and-seek," whispers Heear, jumping out of the mountain of potatoes. Without taking her eyes off the bathroom door, she convinces the little boy to collaborate and stay covered among the tubers. The bathroom echoes with grunts and destructive noises down the hall, which tells Heear that the Buggane is still busy, so she takes the opportunity and stacks the scattered potatoes to try and keep the boy out of sight. The boy inside the pile of potatoes doesn't understand the severity of the situation and lets out a boisterous laugh full of overwhelming anticipation. "Shhhh, hush! You have to be quiet if you want to win the game!"

As the boy promises not to make any more noise, the sounds inside the bathroom stop, and Heear and the pigs feel the Buggane's glowing eyes watching them from inside the dark bathroom interior.

"Sure, you guys can run,

But I know the end has begun."

Heear turns around, showing her back to the hungry creature, and just before running into the cafe, she slaps her furry butt cheek and extends an improper challenge; "Rhyme these, Buggane!" and starts running out of the monster's sight.

The group of escapists hiding in the cinema see Heear running down the aisles and coming their way, followed closely by the two pigs hovering over the sheep's head. Shiar snorts, rolling her eyes and asks, "Can we put a leash on that booger?"

"I'm on it," says Johnny, sticking his torso out of the theatre just in time, catching the unsuspecting Heear. The two pigs following her hide inside the sheep's backpack as the human reunites the fairy sheep with her sisters inside the theatre. Betty then grabs a bag of crisps from Heear's backpack, and hearing the Buggane approaching at full speed, throws the crisps in the hallway past the movie theatre, creating a fake trail of food that goes into the souvenir shop inside the building. As she does this, everyone takes cover before the Buggane prowls past them and into the gift shop.

"What were you thinking?" whispers Shiar with bulging veins on her forehead, scolding the piggish sheep.

"Classic Shiar, always making faces for everything. Relax, girl; you're gonna pop something. I have just what you need," says Heear as she introduces Shiar to the fairy pig she just saved. "Look, I found him in the bathroom, but now you're in charge of him." The fairy pig begins to flutter around Shiar, and her bitter face lights up immediately when she sees the beautiful pig playing near her. "But if you're not sure you want to bear the responsibility, I'm sure Twoaie would be happy to—"

"Don't you dare! If you take him away from me, I… I…"

"You'll ram him!" suggests Jiass, teasing another of the little pigs.

"Yes! Thank you. If you dare, I'll ram you," she assures, dropping to the floor to play with the fairy pig.
"Ok, it's official," says Twoaie smiling, seeing Heear's plan take effect. "We broke Shiar. Now what?"

"Now you all cry,
Pray to the sky,
'Cause you're gonna die,
So say goodbye!!!"
The Buggane's voice can be heard as his head appears behind the cinema's threshold with fierce eyes and a growling stomach.
Johnny jumps in front of Betty instinctively, shielding her from danger, and all the other magical creatures decide to use the mortals as a cover.

"Give me the pigs, and I'll let you run for the hills and save your wife,
The magical game is mine; I have already sharpened my knife."

"Don't talk about me like I'm sitting on a shelf,
This wife has no problem taking care of herself."

"Woman! How dare you? Are you not afraid?
You should, because under each nail, I have a blade."

"I'm not, because I'm a superb cook and can offer you a brilliant deal.
Nothing compares with this queen's grill.
You haven't lived until you try my meal.
For you, it will be like a steal,
By the time I'm done, you'll be clapping like a seal.
So Mr Buggane, my friend, don't cry, don't squeal,
Just let this boss take the wheel."

The Buggane suddenly freezes, intrigued by the human's

response, daring him to dance.
"I offer you blade,
And you offer me aid?"

"That's how we roll around here.
In Hop-tu-Naa, we prefer to cheer,
Not to run around with a spear.
After all, on the island, every life is dear.
I'm not nagging or pulling your ear,
Instead, let me offer you pie and a local beer."

"Woman, what are you proposing?
Be careful with what you are disclosing.
This here is not just for posing,
You all could end the night decomposing."

Betty responds as only a delightful host would, inviting the Buggane to sit on one of the leather chairs in the cafe.

"Mr Buggane, dear, no need to bite or shed a single tear.
Let's change the gear and steer this party into the clear.
The food in this cafe is like from a magical sphere,
I'll give you a meal you'll remember until next year."

In seconds, Johnny offers the Buggane the best cider on this side of the seven kingdoms. The magical creature wets his whiskers in seven cold foamy pints, gobbling down the elixir as fast as the human can pour it.
Betty enters the kitchen, and in seconds, delicious smells waft from the oven, filling the cafe's atmosphere with aromas that make the hungry Buggane salivate and convince him to wait for the promised reward.

"Little ones, listen, I know that nobody asked,

And the last thing you want is to listen to my jaws blast.
After all, I know I made you feel harassed.
The new day will bring the end to the Hop-tu-Naa forecast,
By one a.m., the bridge between kingdoms will be a thing of
the past,
And, lads, dangers for magical folk in this mortal realm are
vast.
I advise you to move and get the fairy pigs fast."

Twoaie, Shiar, Jiass and Heear know the Buggane is right;
one a.m. on 1st November marks the end of the magical
cycle bringing the kingdoms closer together, at which point
the little fairy pigs risk being trapped on this side of the
bridge for a year.

"The starving madman—I mean—Mr Buggane is right; we
must keep looking. We have to hurry!" says Twoaie,
gathering her three sisters into a circle of confidants. "Do
you know what that means?"

"That all this effort makes no sense because life is nothing
but a cruel roulette of uncertainty with an expiration date,
that we're all going to die, and everything you love ends up
turning into poop?" says Jiass, anxious as always.

"Hey, language! Don't say that kind of thing in front of the
little ones," scolds Shiar as she covers the ears of the fairy
pig next to her.

"Nope," sighs Twoaie, regretting asking. "Divide and
conquer, Jiass, but thanks. We need to split up and quickly
comb this place. It's late, and we need to get to the bridge
before one a.m. in the middle of this storm."

The four Loaghtan fairy sheep disperse, leaving the humans
in the company of the Buggane, who is slowly falling in love
with the magical drink that the man pours into his glass.

"And you say that you make this?
I'm not going to lie; I was coming with a hiss.
I was afraid your drink would taste like piss,
But instead, it's like drinking pure bliss,
Like ambrosia's kiss, refreshing your lips.

And what I smell, are those the works of the miss?"

Johnny follows the Buggane, who expects a full glass at all times, as he moves towards the kitchen, attracted by the variety of delicious aromas wafting through the cafe.
"That's right, that's Betty in the kitchen working her magic…
But on the spot, the only thing that I can think rhymes with that, is 'tragic'."

"Agreed,
Tragic indeed,
So let me proceed.
Do you want a lead?
I know what you need.
Let me get you up to speed.
For me, it's not a difficult deed,
Consonant poetics is what I breed.
To grow the rhyme like a good weed,
You lack the thing I call 'a solid seed'.
Something that leaves room for a big plea,
A 'word' with possibilities to grow like a tree,
Think of terms with sweet endings, like good mead.
Start thinking about the sound of the words with greed,
Without a doubt, I can promise that you will exceed.
One day your head will find that heavenly feed,
Something to help you gain good speed,
Just be careful not to get a nosebleed.
And just like that, soon you will see,
Words will flow like sweet tea,
Or like the beautiful blue sea.
If you achieve, believe,
You will receive,
And supersede,
Guaranteed."

"Oh! I see… so that's the secret…" Johnny walks into the

kitchen with his head spinning, and together with their guest, they find the woman working her magic.

"Right on time; glad you're here! I'm gonna need a hand to get this out of the oven; it's the biggest pie I've ever baked." Betty opens the oven door, and a cloud of aromatic steam blows into the Buggane's beard, who can't believe what his nose is sniffing.

"Let me stand,
And give you a hand."

The burly Buggane leans over the giant pot that Betty has used as a mould to assemble a colossal Hop-tu-Naa pie, and the smells again jolt all the magical creature's senses.

"You must teach me how to cook,
Did you learn it from a book?
Do you have it hidden in a nook?
Let me take a quick look."

Betty blushes with the Buggane's comments and praise and, removing the pie from the mould, explains herself.

"No book, my grandmother taught me.
She used to cook it for tea,
And we ate it by the sea.
Whenever I eat them, I want to dance like a bee,
They remind me of grandma and make me feel free.
I like to think that love is the key.
But it's not something that can be taught on a spree.
Whenever you want, you can return to see.
My kitchen will always receive you with glee.
Here you can relax, learn and take a knee,
You will never have to flee,
No need to behave like an escapee."

The Buggane cackles to Betty's rhymes as she and Johnny lift the large tray they used as a plate to serve the promised snack. The Hop-tu-Naa special makes the table legs squeak under pressure, a gigantic meat pie surrounded by mashed potatoes and mushy peas, all drenched in steaming gravy. Before Johnny can offer him cutlery, the Buggane sits down in front of his colossal pie and sinks his teeth into it.

Meanwhile, Heear, Twoaie, Shiar and Jiass run like crazy from here to there, rescuing little fairy pigs from every hidden corner of this cafe. Finally, after their frantic search, the four Loagthan find 13 fairy pigs and tuck them away inside Heear's backpack, warm and comfy, ready to rejoin their mother.

"Ok, ladies, great job! I think we're ready to go."

"Oh please, Twoaie. You and your eternal positivity aren't fooling anyone. It's past midnight. Do you know how long it'll take us to get to the bridge?"

"If we can even go down in this storm," says Heear. The distracted comment rolls off her tongue as she listens to music and gently dances absentmindedly, lulling the fairy pigs sleeping in her backpack. Yet, she stresses out Jiass even more.

"If the storm doesn't kill us all on the way to the bridge!!" Jiass continues breathing insecurities and worries, anticipating everything impossible to foresee.

"You talking about The Devil's Bridge? I can take you there.

With my belly full, I won't try to bite, I swear.

Oh, don't look at me like that, don't be scared.

I don't like that stare; I am not a bear.

Let me be square; believe me, this is rare.

It's easy; I just need a pear and a chair."

"Here, I have a pear,

This one shines almost with a glare.

And any chair that you need under this roof can be spared."

Johnny smiles, satisfied with his first rhyme, as he rescues one of the few fruits that survived Heear's appetite. The Buggane takes the offering excitedly before clarifying his intentions to the human.

"I'm glad you're not just saying that, my friend,
I hope you are being sincere with your intent.
To save the little ones, we need your consent,
To ensure us a fast and safe descent,
We need to borrow the machine on which you overspend.
The chair with the flare will be a godsend.
And I will give it back when the night comes to an end.
Who knows, maybe without a single bend."

The Buggane makes a face as if he doesn't even believe the lies he is telling the human to get what he wants.
"Wh—What is he talking about?" Johnny can't understand what the magical creature eating the pear for dessert asks of him.

"Love, I'm sorry to be the one to give you this strike,
But I think that what the Buggane wants is your bike."

"What?! NO! Impossible. This is non-negotiable. NO! I'm very sorry, ladies, but I just can't. I just restored it and still haven't taken it for a ride. It's a limited edition…" Johnny's exaggerated tantrum makes him look like a marionette whose puppeteer is having a heart attack. But the fire in his stomach extinguishes when he makes the mistake of shifting his eyes, turning to see the beautiful, magical creatures making their best puppy dog eyes, demolishing the man's emotional defences. Behind them, he notices the Buggane, already trying on motorcycle clothing and other items he found in the cafe's shop, getting ready for the trip down the mountain. "Of course, just what I needed—he has good taste in clothes too. He likes pies and good cider and knows about motorcycles. I hope that he isn't also looking for a guarantor because the insurer won't want to answer my calls after this." He sighs and pauses for a minute. "All right, ladies. I guess that if we're gonna do this, we'll do it with style." Johnny smiles and helps the Buggane, who gets dressed in minutes with all the equipment he needs for the trip. As the cherry on top of the outfit,

Johnny adds the Manx flag as a cape hanging on the beast's back.

Last, the Buggane receives a gift from his hosts; a café race-style helmet and a pair of aviator glasses. Once everyone's ready, they take the bike with the sidecar from the repair shop inside the cafe and place it at the starting line, right behind the garage's closed door.

"Don't be afraid to accelerate it. I'm sure it's built to take the heaviest ride. Just remember to slow down before the corners; they might surprise you!" says Johnny, giving the last bit of advice to the Buggane sitting behind the wheel. At the same time, Betty settles the four Loagthan sheep and the fairy pigs in the sidecar, wrapping them with all the warm and comfortable blankets she could find, plus pies and a thermos full of hot tea for the road.

The rider finally gives a signal, and Johnny hits the button that opens the garage door. As the gate rises, they feel as if the mouth of the storm is slowly opening in front of their faces, barking snow so hard it risks knocking down anyone who isn't anchored to something. The Buggane, surprised by the onslaught of the weather, throws an insecure look at the human, but Johnny smiles back, raising his thumbs with an affirmative gesture.

The Buggane unleashes the machine's fury on the starting line and clings tightly to the fizzing rocket. Ironically, the raucous motorcycle shuts down, demolishing the viewers' expectations of seeing a spine-tingling, energetic outing. It takes the mythical creature several more tries to restart the bike, and finally, its exit from the hangar is convulsive and unsafe, a slow torture for all involved.

The cafe owners even have time to close the garage door and walk to the other side of the building. By the time they peek out the front door, the group is still apprehensively descending the hill and just beginning to roll over the famous asphalt ribbon, approaching the electric rail line.

The magical creatures stop and, for a second, look back to

wave goodbye with friendly gestures to the humans cheering them on in the distance. As the humans wave back, they see an out-of-control electric railway car coming down the hill, descending the snowy peak with its roof ablaze as it leaves long flaming lines behind it. The vehicle is surrounded by what appear to be fairies, punishing a group of mischievous local teenagers trapped inside.

The railroad car whistles past inches from the motionless motorcycle, and for a split second, mythical creatures and humans exchange terrified glances and share faith in the magical, invisible fabric that binds them together.

"Wow!" says Twoaie with a nervous giggle. "Hop-tu-Naa was active this year. I wond—" the sheep stops mid-sentence, feeling the ground lurch beneath her feet.

"Oh no, I knew it. I knew this would happen! The Howl found us; I can feel it!" says Jiass anxiously, pointing to the hill that rises behind the cafe.

The behemoth comes charging at full speed, climbing the summit's hidden face with momentum, and ramps at high speed before landing down the hill in a tangled descent. Despite the apparent chaos with which the spectre moves, there's nothing random about its movements. It takes advantage of its flight time to shift its body configuration, so every time it hits land, it dives into the snow and behaves like a completely different creature.

When the Howl finally reaches the cafe, it jumps over the distillery, flying over the heads of Betty and Johnny, still peeking out the front door. They can see the deformed entity shape-shifting before their eyes, its body formed of a mix of clay, gore, mushrooms and the bones of all the sheep that have met their end in this place. Today, the fallen that are now part of the spirit of this mountain come walking among men, following the scent of the magical creatures that belong to another realm.

Descending the mountain aboard this rocket looks less and less like an adventure for the magical creatures now and more like a fight for survival heading towards Douglas. With no time to lose and the hunter at their heels, the Buggane and the sheep cross the flaming starting line burning rubber, undertaking a duel against the storm, with the mission of reaching the bridge before one a.m. or before the Howl eats them alive.

With their faces sticking out the front door, Betty and Johnny realise they've been holding their breath for a few seconds and finally inhale and look at each other.

"Well… the night is still young; we could still get home aboard that UFO I was telling you about," says Johnny with a nervous smile as he examines the sky, hoping to find something unusual up there.

"Shut up and get inside," says Betty, laughing. She grabs her partner by the elbow, pulls him into the cafe and closes the door behind them. Helplessly, they just breathe, looking at their reflections as if the glass could protect them from the forces roaming the Isle of Man on nights like this. Finally, they fall onto the sofas in the lobby, and with a heartfelt sigh, they hug each other and end the season of magical celebrations.

"A… a… achoooooooo!" The little boy that Heear hid among the potatoes near the lobby sneezes, and his whole hiding place crumbles around him. Potatoes roll everywhere, and the giggling lad falls to the ground, pleased, playing and making angels among the surrounding tubers.

Johnny turns to look at Betty and, with a tired grimace, asks, "Maybe we should leave this one to the constable?"

"I'm on it!" says Betty, already with her mobile at her ear. But, as it rings, an anxious thought invades her. "Love, do you think the wee ones will get to the bridge on time?"

"With this weather? With that monster chasing them?! I'm not sure, but if something can give them a fighting chance, it is that mighty bike!"

Several miles from the cafe, the mighty motorcycle ploughs through the snow on its escape down the mountain. The fairy sheep and pigs cling to what they can inside the wheeled side compartment as the Buggane battles the elements, staging an agonising balancing act to keep them inside the fickle slippery road, a path blurring under the caress of the snow and the blanket of the night.

Biting her lip and leaning out the window of the compartment they're travelling in, Jiass tries to keep her eyes on the Howl following closely behind them, running down the mountain to the left of the route. She's enthralled by the mysterious magical entity with the mass of a double-decker bus rolling around in the air, transmuting mid-jump. Each time it lands, it gallops, mimicking the physical structure of everything it has consumed. As it does this, the sheep skulls embedded in its muddy back hiss with empty sockets when the wind blows through them, emitting a chilling ghostly chorus.

The Howl leaps at them, projecting its mass skyward, reminding the fairy sheep of the propelled jets fired by fountains, but instead of being a column of water intended for onlooker entertainment, it more closely resembles an apocalyptic battering ram descending from the sky, looming overhead.

"Incoming!!" screams Jiass. Immediately, the four fairy sheep surround Heear's backpack, trying to protect the little fairy pigs barricaded inside.

The pilot yanks the handlebars sharply to the right, throwing the projectile he's driving into the void down the hill, making the ride go from bumpy to intense torture inside a concrete mixer in a heartbeat.

The mass of living debris changes its strategy immediately. It enters the hill, following the motorcycle, emulating an angry ram looking for something to charge. When its horns contact the sidecar, the entire crew thinks the end has come.

The bodywork crumples and the metal tears, squeezing materials against the wheels, enslaved by inertia, that find no excuse to stop turning. Sparks fly, turning the bike into a glittery-tailed comet stumbling down the hill. Despite the mortal blow, the good bones on the old machine are still in one piece and running. The sidecar, however, reduces to almost half its capacity and is a sneeze away from falling apart.

"Douglas ahead!" says Shiar, placing some trust in the clump of distant lights hidden by the storm. "That means the road should be somewhere to our left!" she says, struggling not to lose her scarf. She turns to point over her shoulder and lets out a yelp when she finds The Howl galloping right next to them. However, the behemoth doesn't lounge at them; it runs past them, staring with hundreds of empty eye sockets whistling through the broken glass.

"Oh no, what's going on? Why doesn't it hit us? It isn't doing anything. This isn't right!" says Jiass anxiously, thinking that something worse may come their way.

"Because it got hurt, too," says Heear, putting the backpack full of fairy pigs back on her shoulders. "You can tell; look at it."

"Hmmm, I think you're right; it seems it lost size with that last blow. But I still don't understand, wha—" Jiass' anxiety-riddled rambling is cut short by The Howl's whirlwind of teeth sinking on the roof of the sidecar.

The hunter attempts to swallow the basket full of magical creatures and pulls on it, trying to tear it apart from the motorcycle.

"Stay back, beast!
We are not your feast!"

The Buggane kicks The Howl like a vicious percheron trying to kill and yanks the handlebars to the right, shaking off the giant leech and getting away from its teeth.

The Howl attacks again, its jaws snap shut inches above their heads, and it yanks the roof off, swallowing the top of the sidecar, leaving the sheep exposed to the elements.

The Buggane's overreaction and the sudden detachment of the roof cause The Howl to stumble and plunge into the snow, spinning down the hill.

Unwittingly, the group suddenly bursts onto the road again and finds some stability in their journey. The Buggane makes the most of this opportunity and speeds up on the straight downhill road, inviting them to enter the icy fog.

"Wait! Where are we?" Twoaie tries to get her bearings and confirms her fears. "Oh, sheep! Watch out for the Creg Ny Baa ahead!" Then, as the fairy sheep yells at the rider, the fickle storm blows and clears the mist in front of them, revealing the pub opposite the sharp ninety-degree angle the road takes before descending into the city of Douglas.

The Buggane hits the brakes, but it still takes them a good distance and effort to stop, narrowly avoiding crashing into five chopper-style motorcycles that careless tourists left out in the open. All the bike's passengers' hearts are hammering, yet they can still hear the Howl whistling in the distance behind them with a shriek that gets under their skin.

"Come on! What are we waiting for?" says Jiass, tugging at the sleeve on the pilot's jacket. "It's gonna find us; what are you doing???"

"Mental diarrhoea!
I have an idea…"

The Buganne plants his feet on the snow, activates the front brakes and revs the motorcycle. This prevents the machine from moving forward but allows the pilot to use all that energy to turn the bike 180 degrees in place. In a second, the abandoned choppers are now behind them, yet the Buganne continues revving, burning rubber.

"Girls, I think our knight in shining armour is losing his marbles," says Shiar. "Hey, genius, you're gonna wear it out; we need that tire if we want to get to the bridge on time, remember? The bridge?"

After digging through several centimetres of snow, the rear tire makes contact with the asphalt. The friction has the desired effect, and a dense curtain of white smoke forms behind them, building up quickly. Without delay, the beautiful polluting cloud of carcinogens engulfs the bikes. Soon, even the pub is hidden behind the veil.

The Howl finally jumps out of the field, landing on the road a couple of hundred meters uphill, chewing the remnants of the sidecar's roof and tracking down its prey, which awaits at the bottom of the hill. The rider at the mountain's base even challenges the beast, flashing his lights.

The invitation to duel is clear for The Howl, and it accepts the challenge by growing a compact pair of antlers. Then, it shoots down the road, gaining speed as the asphalt beneath it cracks and rumbles.

The magical creatures see death descending on them like an out-of-control locomotive made of skulls. Then, when it is finally seconds away from charging them, the rubber-evaporating Buggane repeats the manoeuvre.

As if possessed, the bike turns 90 degrees in place, aligning its headlights with the road that continues to descend towards Douglas. Then, abusing his luck, the pilot drops the full weight of his mythical butt on the seat, releases the brakes, and, like a rocket, the motorcycle takes off.

As luck would have it, the Howl doesn't understand what's happening until it's too late to change its course and falls into the trap. It tries with desperation to make the sharp turn to follow the motorcycle as its claws frantically try to grab the magical creatures before they escape. At the last second, it sinks a talon into one of the sidecar's tires as the conscious mishmash of corpses, clay and moss slams into the smoke screen that hides the teeth in the Buggane's trap.

The sidecar manages to escape from the duel with a torn tire and the speed and manoeuvrability of a kite trying to make a sharp turn. But, regardless of their good luck, a handful of meters down the road, the tire gets tired of rolling and falls off, defeated by the road, abandoning the basket that convulses on the tarmac. The rescue party of magical pigs feels aboard an old mower dragging and grinding its butt against the landscape, and while it's true that it's the fastest mower this side of the seven kingdoms, it's far from the speed that this escape effort begs for.

The impact of The Howl against the motorcycles hidden in the plastic mist generates a light shockwave that blows and dilutes the veil, revealing the dark entity impaled on the frames of the five machines and embedded in internal combustion engines; troublemaking conditions.

"I think that was it, my friends. I think we beat it!" says Heear as she puts cups of tea in the custody of all her companions. "A cuppa here, a cuppa there, a nice cup of char in every hand," she says, pouring hot tincture from the thermos that Betty packed with classic local friendliness. "A little bit of char three times a day keeps the heart happy and the bones strong."

"That's right, the bones, but I'm afraid also the breath!" says the shy Jiass, beginning to unwind. Then, with some positivism, she raises her convulsive cup, splashing tea, toasting the health of her peers.

As they celebrate, a heavenly contraption, a transcendental object made of magic and matter, pushing the limits, corrugating what is possible with multiplicity, leaps into the race to pursue them. The Howl, having combined with the five bikes, has become a misshapen, shifting amalgamation of vehicles interconnected by a web of magical organic matter. What was once the whistle of a ghostly choir has become the furious roar of war, sung with motorised ram skulls.

"Oh, that's just brilliant! The genius Buggane taught The Howl to use the human machines!" says Shiar angrily and throws her cup of tea at the pilot's helmet. "Now we're gonna kick the bucket for real."

"Hey, it's not that bad. I mean, look at the bright side; at least now you can really hear it coming in the distance." Twoaie tries to drink her tea as if nothing is wrong, but the nervous grimace gives her away. "It's like putting a bell on the necklace of a Hellcat, a civic duty; someone had to do it, if not for the well-being of the youngest in the community, for—"

"It's like putting a Band-Aid on a volcano about to explode, that's it! It doesn't work for a damn thing, girl! What are you talking about?" yells Jiass, shaking her friend by the shoulders.

"Demon of a thousand forms!
Girls, hold on to your horns!"

Performing one last 'Hail Mary', the poet fishes Heear out of his backpack, yanks her out of the side cart and sits the fairy sheep on the motorcycle tank, right in the space between the rider's seat and the handlebars. He quickly repeats the manoeuvre until he rescues everybody from the side cart and accommodates them aboard the central chassis.

"You old sack of worms,
I hope this really burns."

The rider invokes his supernatural strength, throwing a powerful claw into his own vehicle. Then, with a couple of sparkling slaps against the reinforced metal, he severs the weak link between the bike and the sidecar, preparing the hook and bait for the monster to swallow.

The Howl, embodying death, descends upon them with lightning speed, disjointing its jaws open, preparing to swallow them whole as it closes its thousand eyes.

Just in time, the Buggane releases the sidecar, which at this point only serves as ballast, and the crate flies out to meet The Howl's embrace like a phone booth fired from a cannon. The metal basket blows up one of the choppers trapped in the Howl's anatomy, splitting its misshapen body in two. However, the parts never stop moving, and though it loses some coordination and momentum, it manages to stay on the run.

The fleeting angel loses its anchor, regains its wings, and can now propel them over the horizon. The Buggane speeds freely, taking this fight to the city streets. But The Howl is still on the prowl, now made up of two entities, each abusing two engines.

"For the love of god! Now you doubled the threat!" Of course, Shiar finds time to complain despite the urgency of the situation. "Hey! On whose side are you on, mate?"

"Stop complaining; at least you're still alive.
If you don't like it, I invite you to drive."

The Buggane lifts Shiar up by the scarf and sits her right between Heear and the handlebars, putting her in charge of steering. He uses his free hands to capture a stop sign as they drive past it, uprooting the post as if it weren't firmly planted on the pavement. Next, with Olympic precision, he throws the javelin from his saddle, impaling the nearest machine and taking another engine out of this race, forcing the Howl to assimilate the three remaining engines into a single entity, concentrating its power for the last stretch.

"I don't want to be snappy,
But I hope you're happy!"

At the stroke of one a.m., the eye of the storm shifts, gravitating towards Peel, and in Douglas, the weather event is finally losing its vibrancy. Nevertheless, the pilots still feel the urgency running through their veins, that golden line on the goal prompting them to accelerate.

The Buggane grabs anything he can throw at his pursuer, from fire hydrants to pillar boxes, dismembering the threat one explosion at a time until they finally shake off the demon, leaving its magical remains scattered through the city.

The clock is ticking, so the group ploughs on; there's never time to stop to smell the flowers or enjoy the triumphs. A few minutes later, they slowly make their way across the uneven countryside terrain, trying to stay close to the river until the Devil's Bridge finally welcomes them.

As they approach, the rock arch that has seen water pass from time immemorial reacts to its magical citizens. The stone cools down to reach super-conductivity, lighting up the symbols hidden in its cracks and opening the magic gate that promises to take them to the cosmic intersection between realms. The magical event lights up the place with the glow of a stadium burning neon, giving the impression that what is taking place could be seen from the moon without the slightest effort.

"Last stop,
Time to hop!"

The Buggane stops in front of the paranormal portal, leaving his passengers at the foot of the inter-dimensional affair. He even cares to help them gently dismount from the overheated machine.

"Thanks for the trip, my friend," says Twoaie, struggling to find the words to show her appreciation towards the creature. "I don't know how we would have done it without your help."

"It's true; we'd probably still be coming down the mountain!" says Heear, examining the little fairy pigs sleeping safely inside her backpack with a smirk.

"You wish! We would be going down the mountain all right, but inside The Howl's belly! So I propose a toast to the health of the Snaefell Buggane, who, against the clock, took us to safe dock." says Shiar, raising her teacup.

"And what are your plans now, my friend?" asks Twoaie

"After this drop,
I'll return to the shop…

Guess the human won't be happy about the lost top."

Says the Buggane, patting the tank, diverting attention to Johnny's machine, trying not to deal with his own emotional conflicts.
"Oh, nothing a good polish can't fix! Right, girls?" The fairy sheep's inside joke makes no sense to the Buggane, who decides not to overstay his welcome and departs.

"End of the show,
It's time for me to go,
And for you, an opportunity to grow."

Says the Buggane, directing everyone's attention to the portal that starts showing signs of weakness as one a.m. approaches.
After fighting her insecurity for a few seconds, Jiass asks, "Mr Buggane? If you have nowhere to go, maybe you'd like to join us…" But the machine has taken him away from their lives the same way he came into them, amidst noise and confusion.
"Ok, girls, come on, let's cross the finish line. Let's get these little ones back home; their mum must be worried si—" Twoaie's tongue trips over her thoughts as she notices that it's getting harder and harder to lift her legs to move forward, competing against the muddy ground beneath her hooves.
"Mate, I think something strange is happening…"
"Oh, no, no! This can't be. This can't be happening!" says Jiass, on the brink of a panic attack. "This is it. It found us; we're done!"
Skulls emerge from the mud around them and just below them, forcing them to step on the empty sockets that answer their questions with the eerie hiss of dead prayers. No matter what you do, The Howl, akin to death, always catches up with you in the end.
The jaws of the mountain reform around them, weaving a cage next to the devil's bridge to swallow them alive. Then,

amid their darkest moment, the answer to their prayers returns, approaching with a distant roar.

The Buggane speeds up, gaining as much speed as the battered bike allows, and ramps on a large rock next to the river. He jumps and dismounts just in time, abandoning the machine that takes flight and crashes into the living maw trying to chew the magical creatures. The resulting explosion blows a small hole in the mouth of hell, giving the sheep an unexpected way out.

"Don't wait for the sun,
Get up and run!"

Taking advantage of the momentary confusion ringing in The Howl's consciousness, the fairy sheep escape out of its mouth and run toward the dying flickering portal, leaping into the light that unceremoniously swallows them.

The Howl tries to follow them before the portal is completely extinguished, but it's stopped by the gigantic river stones the Buggane throws at it without rest or mercy.

Furious, the macabre entity invokes all the surrounding inert matter it can possess, gaining size, widening, taking an increasingly aggressive posture, surpassing the Buggane's size and power by far. Despite this, the poet doesn't miss the opportunity to kill time and distract The Howl, chattering away.

"Have you heard about the Corlett twins and the Whisper Fairy,
And the Hop-tu-Naa night that was quite scary?"

Receiving no coherent response from the confused poltergeist, the Buggane continues;

"Ok, one moral of the tale,
Is how you can bite the evil's tail.
Sometimes, you just have to play snail,
Until time finishes burning its veil,
Taking, with it, the trail."

The hands of the clock finally reach one a.m., marking the end of Hop-tu-Naa. The worlds begin to move apart once more, weakening the connection between both realms. The portal under the devil's bridge quivers until the flame in it goes out, closing the magic passage permanently, at least for now.

"Hold on until the storm blows away;
This is how the small, frail prey
Ends up being the one who saves the day."

Determined to take down its rival, The Howl charges in on the hero with the power of an avalanche and a deafening shriek coming out of its multiple skulls. As it darts towards the Buggane, it slowly crumbles in agony over the river, betrayed by the divine designs that have written the rules of this plane. The magical forces that possess and create The Howl also fade with the arrival of a new day, and with its last breath, it gets close enough to leave a dried-up sheep's skull nibbling at the Buggane's boot.

The so-desired calm and peace arrive suddenly, extinguishing in a heartbeat the event that seemed to illuminate the entire island, plunging the victor into the shadows of oblivion, just like every glorious hero that has ever existed.

The Buggane rubs his tired eyes and blinks a few times, not entirely sure what he sees. The skull at his feet seems to glow faintly, with an almost imperceptible throb he can't ignore. He knows he will regret doing this, but still, he bends down and lifts the skull with a grunt, peeking into its empty sockets.

From inside the chalky skull, the Buggane rescues what appears to be an unconscious little fairy, breathing faintly. The victor's empty stomach rumbles inside his belly, filling his head with ideas he doesn't hesitate to act on, and he gets lost in the darkness surrounding him as he rambles on.

"I'm starving, not gonna lie,

I wonder if it's too late to go for a pie?
Come with me, little one, don't be shy,
I know a good cafe where we can get dry,
A brilliant place up high, close to the blue sky,
Where everyone is seen respectfully in the eye.
Yessir! Victory Cafe rules; I will forever testify!"

Printed in Great Britain
by Amazon